Second Best Friend

Second Best Friend

Non Pratt

Barrington Stoke

First published in 2018 in Great Britain by
Barrington Stoke Ltd
18 Walker Street, Edinburgh, EH3 7LP

www.barringtonstoke.co.uk

Text © 2018 Leonie Parish, writing as Non Pratt

A CIP catalogue record for this book is available
from the British Library upon request

ISBN: 978-1-78112-757-5

Printed in China by Leo

For Beef & Liberty

1

Dumping Rob King

Rules for breaking up with the hottest guy in school.

1. **Know your reasons**
2. **Look fierce**
3. **Take your best friend for moral support (even if she puts up a fight)**

"It's not like I'm going to be there when you do it, creeping up behind Rob, giving you a thumbs-up and whooping, 'You go girl!'" Becky says. She's sitting on my bed, the back of her hand a rainbow of colour from testing all the different eyeliners I've tried and rejected for tonight's look.

"But could you?" I ask. "Because that would be awesome."

"Jade ..." Becky pleads, and I turn from my reflection to look at her.

"Please," I say. "I need you."

"I didn't exactly come prepared for a night out." She holds out the hem of her giant *Adventure Time* T-shirt. It's old and faded and covered in moth holes.

"Good job we're the same size," I say. Same everything, pretty much. Same golden blonde hair, same height, same style.

I reach into my wardrobe and pull out a galaxy-print cami that Becky's borrowed so many times it may as well be hers. She looks unsure.

Time for the big guns.

There's a tangle of necklaces hanging over the corner of my mirror and I hook out my favourite – laser-cut acrylic planets on a silver chain.

Becky looks from the necklace to my hopeful expression and rolls her eyes.

I win.

✗

It's standing room only in the bit of the cinema that can't decide whether it's a bar or a coffee shop. Becky and I push past the popular lot on the leather sofas, and find some space by the window where Willow from orchestra is chewing a straw and guarding a pile of bags and coats dumped at her feet. She's wearing a bright yellow tennis dress and purple satin bomber jacket – the kind of outfit only someone with Willow's deep brown skin and sky-high confidence could ever carry off.

"Cute necklace!" Willow says. She stops chewing her straw long enough to wave it at Becky.

"Thanks, it's Jade's ..." Then Becky stage whispers, "... *for now.*"

The look I give Becky makes it clear that 'for now' means 'for ever'. Becky might be my favourite person, but that doesn't mean I'm prepared to give her my favourite necklace.

"Heads up." Becky nudges me. The lads are on the move from where they've been messing around at the counter.

"Jade!" Coxy, the loudest of the lot, directs to Becky, then he turns to do his trademark finger-guns at me. "Becky!"

"You're hilarious," I say.

He isn't, but it's routine for him to make the joke and me to be sarcastic about it. Not that it matters – like the rest of his mates, Coxy has turned to talk to Becky and Willow, leaving me to face Rob King, my soon-to-be ex.

4

Rob slips a hand under the hem of my top, his fingers tracing a line across the skin of my back as he murmurs, "Looking good, Jade."

If you'd told me a month ago that Rob King, a boy so hot he should be measured on the Scoville scale like a tasty little chilli pepper, would touch me like this, I'd have melted into a puddle of lust. I mean, he's *gorgeous*. Dirty blond hair brushed up into an effortless, scruffy quiff, cute smile and a dimple to die for.

All things best admired from afar. Get any closer and you discover his moves are cut and pasted from a '*How to Make Girls Fancy You*' Wikihow, the quiff is more product than hair and, after he's had a beer or two, that cute smile is a cover for some epic fish breath.

"Let's go somewhere quiet," I say, hooking my fingers with his.

I glance back to see Becky mouth, *"You got this!"* as Rob and I weave our way around the crowd from school and towards the darkened doorway of a fire exit.

As Rob dives in like a haddock on heat, I twist away so all he gets is my cheek.

"Everything OK?" He brushes aside a strand of hair that's fallen from my pony-tail and gives me his Serious Eyes.

When you're as fit as Rob you *really* shouldn't have to try so hard.

"Not really," I say, then let everything out on the next breath. "This has been fun, and you're gorgeous and all, but I'm just not feeling it."

"Feeling what?" Rob has a funny little smile, like he's not taking me seriously.

"This." I wave at the space between our bodies. "Us."

Rob's face stays the same – the puckered brows, the patronising smile – but there's a tightness to it as his humour pulls back. Like a bow tensed before the arrow is fired.

"*You* aren't feeling *us*?" Rob asks. Before I can reply, he shrugs and steps back. "Whatever. Like there would ever have been an 'us' if your mate had been up for it."

I stand there, too stunned to process what he's saying. Which mate? Up for what?

"What do you mean?" I manage.

"Everyone knows Becky's the hot one." Rob reaches up to pat my cheek and I slap his hand away. He laughs, a nasty hiss through his teeth. "Everyone except you, Jade."

2

Certain Qualities

In Monday's Science lesson, Raji Grover reaches across to write in the margin of my worksheet – *Heard you broke up with Rob?* ☹

I reply with the happiest face I can draw. Then I circle it three times. And add an exclamation mark. On my other side, Becky pokes me with a pencil and nods at Dr Foong, who's frowning over at our bench.

"What's the Rob chat, then?" Raji asks as we head out of the lab. "I would say your loss is girl-kind's gain, but ...?"

Raji is one of the popular lot and a few of them draw closer to hear my answer.

"Depends," I say. "How do you feel about kissing someone who snogs like a sloppy smoked mackerel?"

I sculpted that insult on Saturday and my patience is rewarded by a lot of gagging and a repulsed "Ew!" from Raji.

"Pretty on the outside, fishy on the inside," I add, and we all break down into gleeful cackles. All except Becky.

"Should you really be spreading rumours like that?" Becky asks as we part ways with the others at the bottom of the stairs.

"Is it a rumour if it's true?"

"I'm just saying." Becky looks pretty even when she frowns. "It's bad manners to bad mouth someone when you're the one who did the dumping."

She's right – and normally I wouldn't – but what

Rob said *hurt*. All weekend it's played in the back of my brain like muzak turned up a bit too loud to ignore. I can't even look at Becky without hearing Rob say "... *if your mate had been up for it.*"

The truth is that Becky's not up for it with anyone, but I only know that because she's my best mate. She's not someone who reveals much of herself to the rest of the world. The only way for Rob to find out would be to try it on with her – so when was that? The night he got with me there was a big crowd out and it's not like I was glued to Becky's side all night ...

The thought of Rob trying his Wiki-moves on my best mate before lowering his aim to me is shameful. And yet I can't bring myself to check with the one person who could confirm if it's true. There are some things better left unsaid, even to your best mate.

It's almost a relief to split from Becky for the next lesson.

Our school's part of some government scheme that's supposed to teach us how to adult. So Mondays, Wednesdays and Fridays our form has Social Responsibility, Bravo Form does Household Enterprise and the Charlies have Exam Skills. Even though we have the exact same subject, Becky and I have been assigned to different rooms. For once.

As I walk into class, I see Willow waving me over to where she's nabbed a seat next to the radiator. On my way over I catch the tail end of what they're saying about me on the back row.

"... been slagging Rob off because he dumped her," Coxy almost bellows.

"Fake news!" Willow manages to drown Coxy out. "*Jade* is the one who dumped *Rob*. Stop getting your mouth confused with your arse, Matthew Cox."

Thankfully the teacher arrives before things kick off. Mr Wilkinson *five-four-three-two-ones* us into silence then jumps up to sit on the desk, flashing us the yellow sole of his navy brogues. He might be my dad's age, but Mr Wilkinson dresses like an ASOS advert.

This term we're working towards a school election. Our class are the Wildcats and Becky's are the Honey Badgers. Last lesson, Mr Wilkinson talked about what a Campaign Manager does, using a slide of characters from TV shows our parents might have watched back in the day, but mean nothing to us.

Today, it's about the Party Leader, and he's decided to play it safe.

"Who's that then?" Coxy shouts, thinking he's clever.

"Even you know what the Prime Minister looks

like, Matthew," Mr Wilkinson says. "I assume it's because you're so far back you can't see. Move to the front, please."

Coxy groans and moves to sit next to Nick Pallis – who looks just as thrilled. Once Coxy's settled, Mr Wilkinson divides us into groups to discuss what qualities a Party Leader should possess.

"This is bullshit." Coxy leans back in his chair, scowling at me, Willow and Nick like it's our fault. "Someone should tell Wilko this lesson's meant to be a doss."

"Every lesson's a doss for you, isn't it?" I say. I flash him a grin, forgiving him for what he said before. Coxy's best if you don't take him seriously. "Even you can think up something our leader should have."

"Good looks." Coxy points to his own face

without a hint of irony. "Skin fit for a billboard and a shit-eating grin."

"What else?" I ask, writing down 'good looks' since I'm the only one holding a pen.

"Charisma," Nick says, then starts to spell it until I death-stare him into silence. Nick's all right – a smart arse who thinks he's cooler than he is, shirt a bit unbuttoned, tie a little loose ... and a School Council badge pinned to his jumper.

"Can we think of anything less shallow?" Willow looks disgusted with what we've come up with so far.

"Integrity?" I say. "You want someone who stands by their beliefs."

"Someone who can hold their own in an argument," Willow adds. "Who won't fluff their lines in a debate."

"Yeah, Nick," I say, darting a glance up at him.

"One time, Stickland," Nick replies. "One time."

Both of us were on the Debate Team last year when we fluked our way into the semi-finals of a big competition. It was Nick's job to give the vote of thanks to the opposition, but he got the name of their school wrong. We didn't make it to the finals.

"What about knowing how to organise people without pissing them off?" I suggest.

"You mean diplomatic?" Nick says, his grin hitched up to reveal the canine tooth he chipped when he fell down the stairs in the science block. "Need me to spell that one for you?"

This earns him another death stare, offset by the hint of a smile. As I said, Nick's all right.

Nick sits back in his seat, a smug look on his face.

When we've done our list and the boys have turned to face the front, Willow gives me a knowing look and whispers, "You literally just broke up with Rob."

    I shrug like I don't know what she means, then I sneak a look at the back of Nick's head and smile. Life is more interesting when there's someone to flirt with.

3

Going Solo

Me, Becky and Willow all walk down to the
rehearsal hall together. We're the only three in
Year 11 who still go to orchestra and we like to
grumble about it.

"It'll look good on our personal statement,"
Becky says. Which is a very Becky thing to say.
She's always looking ahead to a future I can't even
imagine, let alone see.

"Either of you signed up for a solo?" Willow asks
as she sweeps her braids over her right shoulder.
There are streaks of maroon running through some
of them and it looks amazing.

There's a music festival next month and Miss Cortez is desperate to put up some soloists against her old school. So far none of us have been keen. I've only stuck with orchestra because of an argument I had with my dad after he made one too many jokes about my "commitment issues". He thinks I give up when things get hard and playing the flute for another year of orchestra was the easiest way to prove him wrong.

"Incoming." Becky murmurs a warning as Rob splits from a group further down the corridor. He's headed our way.

Clark Academy is a big school and this is the first time I've seen him since Saturday.

I keep my attention fixed on my friends and the three of us sail down the corridor as if we're the only ones using it. At the last moment, once Rob's already past, I glance back – low, subtle, pretending to adjust the strap of my flute case …

Busted.

Rob locks eyes with me for half a second, then his gaze moves smoothly on to Becky. His lips curl up in a way that makes me sick.

"Jade?" Willow's at the door to the hall. I hurry in, angry with myself for giving Rob a chance to make me feel like this.

I'm distracted for the whole practice. I *should* be thinking about what the other flutes are up to, but I can't keep my eyes off the string section, where Becky sits, violin tucked under her chin, mouth pursed as she focuses on the music.

Everyone knows Becky's the hot one.

Hot.

Hot.

Hot.

"Stop!" Miss Cortez slashes her hands in command and everyone halts in a messy, tuneless crash. She stands and stares at us in despair. "Have any of you even picked up your instruments in the last seven days?"

Out of the corner of my eye I see Becky shrug one shoulder the way she does when she's the only person in class to have done her homework.

"Again." The way Miss Cortez says it, the word sounds more like a sigh.

This time I'm determined not to lose my focus. I look at the music and take control of my pace, despite the Year 9s rushing through each bar like they're in a race against the rest of us. We go over the middle of the piece a few times before Miss Cortez is satisfied.

"That'll do for today, but before you go …" Miss Cortez lifts the sign-up sheet for solos. It's blank. I meet Willow's eye where she's sitting with the rest of the violins and smile. "I need some soloists," Miss

Cortez says, "and since none of you are going to volunteer, *I* am forced to choose."

As if by magic, everyone looks to the floor, their feet, the view outside the window – anywhere except the music teacher. Who's having none of it.

"Everyone in Year 7, please stand up."

About a third of the orchestra stands up. Miss Cortez thinks about it, then picks two winds and a string. Then she makes the Year 8s stand.

It's easy to see where this is going and I tap the keys of my flute. I watch Miss Cortez, listening to the way she assesses each musician, praising them on a technical detail, or a particular performance.

To volunteer for a solo is one thing, but to be *chosen* is another. I imagine what it would feel like to be picked, my embarrassment battling with pride as Miss Cortez praises me. If Becky's the hot one, maybe I could be something else? Maybe I could –

"Year 11s?" The three of us stand up. "Would any of you like to ...?" Miss Cortez pauses, hopeful.

Pick me. *Pick*. Me.

Miss Cortez sighs. "Very well ..."

My heart picks up tempo.

"... Becky!" she says. "Your last exam piece was note perfect."

4

Top of the Class

Thursday is the only day Becky's sister goes straight home from school – which means it's the only day Becky doesn't. The two Conway girls are twins, but for all they share identical genes, they're opposites in every way possible. Stef Conway is the sort of person who cheeks teachers, 'forgets' to hand in her homework and rocks up to school with SHIT shaved into the buzzed half of her head.

Normally I'm happy to have Becky round to mine, ranting at me about her sister's latest rebellion. But today, the best I can do is nod along and say, "Mm."

"I mean, what's she rebelling against?" Becky says. "Seriously. It's not like the mums *ever* tell her off about *anything*."

She has a point. My dad would kill me for half the stuff that Stef gets away with, but then he's as conservative as they come.

He loves Becky.

At the dinner table, Dad treats my best mate like she's fresh back from her gap year rather than someone who stays over so often she has her own toothbrush. There's a lot of school talk and I exchange an eye-roll with Mandy, my step-mum. As far as she's concerned, I'm Matilda to her son's Mr Twit – but tonight there's no Harvey here to make me look better. There's only Becky, who makes me look worse.

"So, Becky, how's school treating you?" Dad tops her glass up and puts the jug down without offering me any. "Jade's acting like it's her final year of university."

"Well, the teachers do keep saying it's the most important year of our lives," Becky tells him.

"See?" I say to Dad, as I blow Becky a kiss across the table.

"Thought it was just you," Dad says, trying to wind me up. "Making a meal out of how hard it is."

"It is hard!" I say, just as Becky says, "I don't think either of us find it that hard."

We look at each other, trying to work out who should explain that one away.

"I mean ..." Becky pushes her food around her plate. When people pay her too much attention, the apples of her cheeks ripen to perfect red circles as if air-brushed onto her face. "It's not hard like *difficult*. Just hard as in more work."

Dad rests his knife and fork on the edge of his

plate as he looks at Becky and me. Then he shakes his head and laughs.

"Well." He pats the back of my hand in a way that's supposed to be affectionate. "Some of us find work harder than others."

"Thanks for that," I mutter, attacking my potato so hard that I fire a load of peas off the side of my plate and onto the floor.

Dad's never been one for taking a hint. Next he moves on to what homework we've done this evening. Mostly our 'homework' has been re-watching the best Dan and Phil videos from 2016. Becky knows my dad won't want to hear that.

"Just something for Social Responsibility," Becky says, unimpressed by the very thought of it. S.R. is the only subject other than Games that doesn't count for anything – no grade, no glory. It's the reason I like it.

"We've got to choose what position to apply

for as part of that election I told you about," I say. "Becky's applying for Researcher and I'm thinking about Media Consultant."

Dad grunts. Like Becky, he thinks anything without an exam at the end is a waste of time.

"And we got our results back in Biology," I add, wanting to show I can do well in something my dad cares about. Riding high on a swell of pride, I say, "I got 64%."

"Brilliant, Jade," Mandy says, lifting her glass and chinking it on mine. "To the next David Attenborough ..."

I'm grinning, but I'm also trying to shrug it off, not wanting to sound big headed.

"How'd you do, Becky?" Dad asks.

There's the tiniest of pauses as Becky glances down at her near-empty plate. "Umm ... 72%," she says.

Later, we're left alone to tidy up and put the dishwasher on. I seethe in silence as I wipe the table down with more force than necessary.

"Have I done something to upset you?" Becky asks. "You've been quiet all evening."

"No," I say, feeling guilty. None of this is her fault. Not really. "Just in a grump."

"Anything you want to talk about?" she offers, shutting the dishwasher and standing up so that I'm forced to look her in the eye.

"Really," I say. "It's nothing."

As I hold my fist out for the One-Potato-Two-Potato Fist-Bump of Friendship, I try to convince myself that I'm telling my best friend the truth.

5

Fantasy

Becky's late to lunch because she has to see Miss Cortez about her solo.

As I wait in line for the water jugs, I think about all the pieces I could have played if Miss Cortez had picked me.

"Can a shadow exist without something to cast it?" a voice says. "Or am I just seeing things that aren't there?"

I'd been so distracted with my musical day dreams that I hadn't noticed Rob approach. The two boys with him snigger at his little joke.

"Miss me so much that you're hallucinating me

now, Rob?" I quip, pleased at how fast the comeback springs from my lips – even more pleased at how Rob's friends snigger at my joke this time.

Rob scowls. It's one of those scowls you might think was sexy if you saw it in a black and white photo, but looks unpleasant and childish when you know the person behind it.

For a moment, I think I've won, until Rob's sneer slides into smug.

"We both know that if I was going to fantasise about someone it wouldn't be you."

I'm too sickened to think of anything sensible to say, but from out of nowhere, a clipped, confident voice says, "Like you ever fantasise about anyone other than yourself, Rob."

My saviour is Becky's sister, Stef. She stands next to me, arms crossed, head cocked, a cascade of lilac hair falling from one half of her head.

Rob's mates burst into activity, slapping him on the back. "Burn, mate! *Burn.*"

"Go on," Stef says, shooing the three of them with a flick of heavily ringed fingers. "Off you fuck."

Rob opens his mouth, grasping for the last word, but Stef is not someone to be messed with. In the end, he's forced to follow the others over to the far corner of the lunch hall.

"Thanks, Stef," I say, and I mean it.

"Whatever." She leans over and pours us both a glass of water. "Family look out for each other. Speaking of which ..."

Stef nods towards where Becky's half way along the line for hot food, then she heads back to sit with her own friends while I wait for mine.

Becky doesn't say anything until we're sitting down.

"What was all that about with Stef?" Becky asks.

There's a particular tone she uses for her sister, one that hints at disappointment and distaste – as if everything Stef does is automatically bad.

"Nothing," I say, not wanting to get into it.

"So long as you remember which Conway twin's the best." She points her fork at me, only semi-joking, then spears one of my roast potatoes.

Perhaps if Rob wasn't leering at us from across the hall, I'd have thought to say something to comfort her.

✗

Mr Wilkinson's mood is as jazzy as his hipster bow-tie when he rocks up to S.R. with the applications we handed in last week. My dad's nonsense at dinner on Thursday annoyed me so much that I binned the application I'd started for Media Consultant and applied for Party Leader instead. So what if Dad doesn't care about S.R.? It's the only subject in which Becky's not around to beat me. The only subject in which there's any point aiming for the top. For once, I really care about doing well.

"Before I return your marked applications, please can you arrange yourselves according to what position you applied for ..." Mr Wilkinson says. "Media over here, Researchers there, Treasurers ... Campaign Managers ... Party Leaders, you guys can go up to the front."

I keep my head down as I push through the crowd of Media applicants to get to the front. I'm ashamed of my ambition now I'm forced to own up to it. There, I join Ollie Woods, captain of the rugby team, and Bogdan Korda, who's smart and serious and wins all the school science prizes. As the dust settles, I stare back at the rest of the class, wondering what's going to happen next. From his seat among the Campaign Managers, Nick Pallis meets my eye and raises his eyebrows like he's a tiny bit impressed to see me up here.

"Our candidates, everyone!" Mr Wilkinson swings round and gestures to me, Bogdan and Ollie.

There's a smattering of applause and some sarcastic cheers as he hands the three of us our applications.

"For all the other positions, I'll choose who will lead each team, but for this one ..." Mr Wilkinson drums his hands on the desk and says in an accent that's meant to be Geordie, "*You decide!*"

Bogdan, Ollie and I exchange startled glances.

"Our candidates will read out the opening statement of their applications. Wildcat party members, listen closely, watch how they perform and think about what you want from the person who will represent your party to the electorate."

Mr Wilkinson clears his throat and turns to Ollie.

"Oliver Woods, if you will?"

I look down at my paper. *Excellent work, Jade* is scrawled across the top. Praise – unfamiliar and thrilling – lights me up. As Ollie blusters his way through his statement and then Bogdan starts up in the drone of someone who hates public speaking, I start to believe I've found something I can win.

At last.

6

Head to Head

Bogdan gets 8 votes, Ollie 10. I get 13.

It's not a landslide, but victory tastes sweet all the same. Back in my seat, I watch Mr Wilkinson sort out the others.

- ✗ Nick (of course) for Campaign Manager

- ✗ Silver Maths Challenger Marlon for Treasurer

- ✗ Natasha – who hangs with the popular lot – for Policy

- ✗ And, much to her disgust, Willow as Lead Researcher

In true political style, Mr Wilkinson saves the controversy for last. Next on his list is –

✘ Coxy as head of the Media team

"*What?* Come on, sir ..." Nick's protest is almost as loud as Coxy's.

Mr Wilkinson ignores them both.

"Matthew Cox has a real talent for getting noticed. Imagine what that talent could do for the party?" Mr Wilkinson taps Coxy on the head with his rolled-up application before he hands it back to him. "Besides, it's about the team, not just the leader. Politics is about policies not personalities."

"Good, because Coxy doesn't have one!" Ollie yells from the safety of the research team.

Once we've simmered down, Mr Wilkinson runs over the election schedule. Next lesson – Friday – there'll be a hustings. For the hustings everyone who can vote (Years 10 and 11) will see the two parties up on stage and listen to a short speech from each party leader.

"Your homework for tonight ..." Mr Wilkinson points to the research team. "Design a short questionnaire to collect polling data ..." He then picks up a sheet and hands it to Marlon. "I want the treasurers to work out how much you'll spend on each part of the campaign within a budget. Media team, please put together some basic visuals for the hustings – rosettes and flags, that kind of thing. Policy people, fine tune the manifesto and work out what points are most important. Nick, work with Marlon and Matthew Cox to make sure materials are printed on time and on budget for the hustings. Jade – once Natasha's sent you the policies, write a one-minute speech to impress the voters."

When the bell goes for the end of the lesson

we're left slack jawed and boggle eyed at the vast amount of work we have to do.

"I'll give you a basic visual on how many fucks I have to give about this," Coxy says to Nick as we leave the classroom. He puts both hands up to form a giant zero before he's round the corner and out of sight.

"What does Coxy not care about?" Becky asks from where she's been leaning against the Year 8 Poetry Display, waiting for me.

"Anyone other than himself," Nick says, as he falls into step with us. Like me and Becky, Nick has English in the library. "Nice one, by the way, Jade."

Nick holds his hand up for a high-five and I slap it half-heartedly as if I'm too cool to take it seriously.

"But, let's face it, I'm the one who'll be doing all the work," he adds, cocking a smile at me.

"Just the dirty work, Nick." The phrase sounds

more suggestive than I intended and earns a prudish frown from Becky. She never approves of how fast my crushes move.

"What are you two on about?" Becky asks, holding the door for a stream of Year 7s as they hurry to the hockey pitch in their games kit.

"Just Jade getting herself voted in as Leader of the Wildcats." Nick high-fives me *again*, then swoops his hand down to dust off his lapels as he adds, "And yours truly being hand-picked as her Campaign Manager."

But Becky's not paying Nick the slightest bit of attention. She's staring at me, mouth open like she's so shocked she's forgotten how to close it.

"Get. Out. *Really?*" I'm still deciding whether to take her surprise as a compliment or an insult when Becky says, "Because I'm Leader of the Honey Badgers."

There's a pin-drop pause.

"For real?" I say.

"For real!" Becky says like it's the best news ever.

I don't know how to arrange my face any more than I know what to say. If there were no one else here then maybe Becky would be able to see how annoyed I am. But Nick is here and he fills what would have been a hurtful silence with real interest, joking about it making headlines in the school paper.

"I thought you applied for Researcher?" I say, cutting across whatever Nick's saying as we enter the library. There's only one free table and all three of us dump our stuff on it.

"I did," Becky says, as she gets her books out of her bag. "But Miss Prasad picked a shortlist of candidates for Party Leader and I was one of them."

Of course she was. Becky doesn't even need to compete to win.

"Not that it matters," she carries on, "everyone's going to vote for whichever party their mates are in."

"Wildcats have some pretty good policies you know," I say. "Stuff people care about –"

"Careful, Stickland," Nick warns from his seat across the table. "As your Campaign Manager I'd advise you not to discuss strategy with the leader of the opposition."

Becky laughs. "Oh my God, you sound like you actually care."

"I want to win," Nick says, like it's not something to be ashamed of.

"And you always get what you want, do you?"

Becky thinks she's being subtle, but Nick sees right through her. He flashes me a self-satisfied smirk that I definitely should not find the least bit sexy.

"Maybe," Nick says, before starting up some chat with one of the other tables.

As I stare at Nick's profile, idly admiring how his Greek genes have given him a pleasing combination of eyebrows, nose and hair, what I'm thinking about has nothing to do with Nick at all.

I'm thinking about Becky. I'm thinking that, yet again, she's going to beat me.

All that effort I put into the application, wasted.

7

New Hair, Do Care

Last night, after Becky left my house, I should have practised my snappy speech for the hustings. But instead I did something else entirely.

"Oh my God – your hair!" Raji Grover yells as I pass her in the corridor.

It's exactly the reaction I wanted and I beam almost as bright as my new red hair. I brush my side-swept fringe out of my eyes and try to tuck it behind my ear. Mandy might be a freelance journalist these days, but she's a trained hairdresser too, which comes in handy when her step-daughter asks for an emergency cut and colour. A crowd gathers around me, showering me with compliments.

"That's well lush, Jade," says Kirsten Brody who sits with me in D.T.

"You look a bit like Emma Stone!" someone behind me says.

"But with normal-sized eyes," Kirsten adds.

"Thank you." I think.

Another girl holds out her phone next to me with a Google image of Emma Stone with a flicky fringe and wavy bob.

"Hair twins!" Raji shouts.

"It's making me jealous," Becky says from where she's been waiting next to a poster for the hustings. But she doesn't mean the hair. She means she's jealous of Emma Stone being my new hair twin instead of her.

I can't tell her that's the exact reason I've done it.

"No need to be jealous, Becks!" Raji says. "Your hair's gorgeous!"

"Why don't you try a parting on the other side?" Kirsten reaches out and flips Becky's hair over – an intimate gesture I know will make my best mate squirm. Just like that, Becky's the one in the spotlight as everyone suggests how she can mix up her hair without the drama of a new cut and colour. And I'm standing there – watching, waiting – and realising *that was it*.

My new hair is old news and Becky's the one making headlines.

In Social Responsibility, Coxy makes a crass joke about where else I might want to try a new hairstyle, but I'm not in the mood.

"Fuck right off," I snap, earning a chorus of "Oooooh" and "Sense of humour fail!"

"Someone nervous about the hustings?" Nick

says, coming to sit on Willow's desk. She doesn't shove him off like she would half the boys in this class. "Because you don't need to be."

I don't say anything. I haven't given the hustings even a second's worth of thought.

"For real, Jade," Willow says, backing him up. "You'll ace this."

I nod. I need to focus if I'm going to ace anything other than being in a bad mood.

As Mr Wilkinson comes in, Nick hops off the desk. He pauses a second, then says, "I like your new hair by the way."

✕

Twenty minutes later and I'm backstage with the other Wildcats, fretting about going on-stage. It's the first time 'the electorate' – everyone in Years 10

and 11 – will hear what the Wildcats stand for. I'm
a bit hazy myself. Natasha emailed me the policy
team's bullet-point manifesto, but I've barely had
chance to skim it. I scroll down the list on my
phone, fighting a tidal wave of panic. There are 350
people out there waiting to hear what I've got to
say ... by now I should probably have some idea of
what that will be.

Marlon peers round the curtain and nudges
Natasha. She whispers to the rest of us that they're
closing the hall doors.

"Your rosette's wonky," Willow says, and she
tugs me closer to re-pin it. It doesn't do much good.
All of the Wildcat rosettes look wonky, no matter
how they're pinned. Rather than get annoyed, like
Nick did when he found out Coxy made them in
registration, I feel reassured that I'm not the only
person on the team who hasn't done their homework.

I tuck my phone into the top of my skirt and re-roll my shirt sleeves. Now I'm fretting about my speech *and* how I look *and* feeling like I need the loo ...

Nick's watching me.

"Don't stress," he says, giving me a thumbs-up. "You look good. More than good."

"Keep it in your pants, Pallis," Coxy says in disgust from where he's sitting on the throne used in last year's *Wizard of Oz*.

"But do I look like a serious political heavyweight?" I say, enjoying the rather cute way Nick's blushing.

"Of course," Nick says at the exact same time Coxy goes, "Nah."

"Because you're not," Coxy adds and Willow reaches over to thump him. "Ow! What was that for? She's not. Becky's the serious one."

👍 Second Best Friend 👍

"Shut it, dickwad," Nick hisses, but it's too late. As Mr Wilkinson calls the Wildcats onto the stage, any last shreds of confidence have deserted me.

8

Rebellion

My performance at the hustings leaves me in
the kind of mood that can't be lifted. Not by the
canteen having curly fries at lunch, not by some
sixth-former saying she loved "that girl's red hair"
as she went past, not by nabbing the front seat at
the top of the bus on the way home. Even pestering
Becky into another night out didn't improve things.
If anything, it's made my mood heavier.

I roll over and look at my best mate. She's
asleep – peaceful, face turned to me, her breath as
soft as a baby's. Becky never notices, but guys check
her out all the time – something I used to take pride

in. Tonight, it just made me feel like crap to watch
a couple of the grammar-school lads mess around on
the Starbucks' sofas, trying to impress her.

Restless, I get up and head down to the kitchen.
It's gone midnight and I take care to be quiet, not
wanting to wake the mums in their own house as I
pad about in the dark. I set myself up with a glass
of milk and a banana, and get my phone out to
check my notifications.

Nick's started following me on Instagram. I
get a stab of excitement at seeing that he's liked
something.

It's a selfie I re-grammed from Becky's account
the night we went to the cinema. Becky and I are
squashed together to fit into the frame, me holding
up a V-salute, winking at the camera as Becky
squishes her lips to the side as if she's about to
plant a bright red kiss on my cheek.

Nick's one of 54 people to like that picture.

There's nothing to be gained from doing it, but still I hunt for the picture on Becky's profile.

114 likes and loads of comments.

@Raj1Gr00v3r Rocking that red lipstick.

@Spexy667Ford added a 100 emoji.

@Kirstennn Hella cute look, B!!! Where's your necklace from??? WANT.

Kirsten's comment fills me with a hot flush of frustration and my thumbs hurt as I hammer out a reply.

@JadedBabe ACTUALLY THAT NECKLACE BELONGS TO M–

"Oh my God, you gave me a heart attack!"

It's Stef, and she is not in her pyjamas. Unless Stef sleeps in hot pants, Timberlands and a tiny *My Little Pony* T-shirt under a huge zip-up hoodie with burn marks on the sleeve.

We both wait a moment to check no one's heard. Then I bend down to get my phone from where I flung it across the table and Stef yanks the fridge open.

"Thank fuck," she mutters. "For a second there, I thought you were Becky."

"Shouldn't I be saying that to you?"

Stef turns to narrow her eyes at me. "Try it."

I do not try it. Stef's clumsy as she digs about in the fridge, swearing when she drops a pizza slice on the floor – which she picks up and puts in her mouth anyway. Cold air and fresh alcohol cling to her clothes as she sits down with a horde of cheese slices and mini chicken satays.

"Bribery." She opens the pack of satays and offers me one. "If anyone asks, I was in by midnight. Sober as a kitten."

"No bribes necessary." But I take a satay stick anyway.

Stef grins. "How would you feel if I replaced my sister with you?"

"Seriously. Can you not?" I say. I know she means it as a compliment, but I can't take it as one. I just can't. "Me and Becky aren't bloody interchangeable."

There's a pause and I can feel Stef staring at me. I focus on the satay stick I'm twirling between thumb and forefinger.

"OK, so I know why I have issues, but, mate ..." Stef starts.

I play with the stick a moment longer. This is my best chance to talk to someone who might get where I'm coming from.

"It's Rob's fault," I say.

"Many things in this world are. Go on." Stef takes another messy piece of chicken from the packet.

"He only went out with me because Becky turned him down."

"No way! Are you for real?"

I shrug. "That's what he said."

"What did Becky say?" she asks.

"Nothing." I press my lips together. "Becky doesn't know he told me."

"Mate ..." Stef blows out a long breath. "What. A. Fucking. Dick."

"Yeah. Well. Now I can't stop noticing stuff."

"About Rob?" Stef asks.

"About Becky. How she's always better than me at everything. She gets better marks than me, gets picked to perform a solo –"

Stef snorts. "You for real? You're pissed that Becky can play the violin better than you?"

I ignore the detail that, in fact, I play the flute. That's beside the point.

"I'm pissed that she can do *everything* better than me." I can hear the whine in my voice. "And I just ... why can't I be the best? Just for a change. Just for one thing. You know?"

Stef puts her satay down on the table and runs her hand across the shaved side of her head.

"It's hard isn't it?" Stef's voice has dropped low, as if she's talking to herself more than to me. "Loving someone so fucking perfect. Like, you love them, because they're your sister – your best mate." She glances up. In the dark of the kitchen, for that second where she's focused on me, it's almost like looking at Becky. "But they're also the competition. The one person you're always measured against."

"Because people see you and they think of her." It sounds like I'm asking, but I'm not. I know exactly what she means.

Stef nods. "Round here it's all gentle sighs and

'Could you not be more like your sister?' eyes."

Becky's voice rings in my ears. *I mean, what's she rebelling against? Seriously. It's not like the mums ever tell her off about anything.*

I look at Stef. I take in her clothes, her make-up, her trademark hairstyle and its ever-changing colour – and the truth seems so obvious that I can't understand why I didn't already know.

It's not her parents that Stef's rebelling against, it's her sister.

9

Like You More

"I know this sounds stupid," I say. And then I stop. However chatty she's feeling, the girl opposite me is still Stefani Conway. She's still *cool*.

"Whatever it is, I won't laugh." She holds up her hand in devil horns. "Drunk girl's honour."

So I tell her about being Wildcat party leader, thinking that I'd won something only to find out I was up against Becky. Again. Any other time Stef would laugh at me for caring about a stupid school election, but not tonight.

"And you think you'll lose?" Stef asks, moving onto the cheese slices now that the satay sticks have gone.

"Did you see me at the hustings?" Even saying the word feels raw.

"Did you think I was paying attention?" is Stef's reply. "Besides, that's like one event – you've got a whole week to campaign before the vote."

"Becky will still win." I shrug. "Being better than me is what she does. It's what she *is*."

Stef goes quiet, ripping her cheese slice into shreds. When she snaps up to look at me, I jump.

"You're wrong, you know." She waggles her cheese at me. "All that other stuff, school and music and whatever is my sister's area of expertise. But an election's about getting people to put their trust in you. It's about being likable."

"Brilliant," I say with zero enthusiasm. "If Instagram's anything to go by I'm about half as likable as your sister."

"Shut right up."

In reply, I open up the phone, deleting my
half-written comment before showing her the two
identical pictures – Becky's then mine.

"One hundred and fourteen to fifty-four. Proof."

"Liking the picture isn't the same as liking
the person," Stef says, missing the whole point of
Instagram.

"It kind of is," I say. "Especially when it's the
same picture."

"I don't get it. The original poster must always get
more likes – if someone follows you both they're not
gonna like it twice, are they?" Stef sees my expression.
"Wow, you really are broken over this, aren't you?
People like you, Jade. *I* like you and I'm really fussy."

My lips twitch in an almost smile, but almost
isn't enough.

Stef watches me a little longer, then takes a
deep breath and places her hands flat on the table.

"Promise that if I tell you something, it goes no further than this kitchen?" she says.

In that moment, we're both aware there's a line that we shouldn't cross.

"Go on," I say, stepping right over it.

"So you know we lived in Wales for a bit?"

I know Becky's family history as if it's my own. Their gran on Mum Maria's side had a stroke and their other mum – Ally, 'Mally' as the twins call her – is a carer. They moved to where their gran lived, a village in the valleys, so Ally could care for her.

"We got there at the end of primary school. Everyone already had friends – they weren't looking to make new ones. Didn't bother me, but Becky struggled. She'd gone from growing up with everyone, to a new school where people laughed at her accent and teased her for speaking up in class. Thought it was weird we had two mums and no dad. You know."

I know, but I don't *know*. Not the way Becky and Stef do.

"Becky always cried on the walk to school, until one day she stopped. I thought that was a good thing, until kids started asking how my sister was doing and telling me how brave she was."

Stef looks at me, her mouth twisted into a shape that's not a smile or a scowl. This conversation has sobered her up.

"My perfect sister ..." It sounds like it's hard for Stef to get the words out. "Told the girl she sat with that she had cancer."

"*What?!*" If it was anyone else saying this I'd have thought it was a wind-up.

"I know." Stef shakes her head as if she still can't believe it. "I don't think she'd ever lied about anything before that. Not really. But Becky was *so* desperate for them to like her."

"What happened?"

"I played along. She's my sister. I pick her side. Always. Even if it's stupid." Stef stacks the cheese slices she's not going to eat in a neat pile next to the empty satay packet. "We told everyone it was this massive secret that they couldn't tell their parents or the teachers. Kids are thick. Funny thing was, it might have stopped Becky from crying on the walk to school, but it stopped her wanting to go home too – in case that was the day one of the kids slipped up. The shame of the lie she'd told ended up worse than having no friends."

"I can't believe she never told me."

"Really?" When Stef looks across at me there's no trace of the sloppiness with which she sat down. "You can't imagine having a secret you're too ashamed to tell your best friend?"

She gets up to put the cheese in the fridge and

tip the satay sticks into the bin, pausing in the doorway to look back at me.

"I'm only telling you this because I know you love her as much as I do." There's concern in the way Stef says it, like she thinks she's said too much. "If you can keep your own secrets from Becky, you can keep that one too."

"Of course," I say. I fiddle with my phone, not able to look her in the eye.

"You think everyone sees Becky the same way you see her, Jade, but they don't. They never have. Not even Becky. She has to work to get people to like her in a way that you don't. Remember that." Stef takes a step out, but turns back to lean round the frame and add, "And remember that if she finds out I told you about the cancer that never was, I'll kill you. Slowly. Painfully. Publicly."

10

Popularity Offensive

What Stef tells me puts a different filter on my memories. It bleaches out everything I took for granted and brings forward things that were lurking in the background. I lie awake so long thinking about it that there's birdsong outside the window before I finally get to sleep.

The next day, I wonder whether Becky can tell that I know something, but of course she can't. It's no different to any other lazy Sunday morning. The two of us are crashed out on her bed binge-watching *Ru Paul's Drag Race* and arguing about which contestant's our Miss Congeniality.

This is Becky's kind of party and the only guest she's invited is me. I'm her person – and Becky doesn't need more than one.

It's weird how I've never understood this until now, but what Stef said about people liking me is true. Before the twins started at our school, I was a drifter. I didn't belong to any particular group, but I got on with all of them. I was never short of someone to sit with in lessons, or at lunch, or on the bus, and I got invited out whenever it mattered.

I still do.

So if Becky's good at school and I'm good at people, I need to treat the election less like homework and more like a popularity contest.

It's time I started my engine.

✗

☞☞ *Second Best Friend* ☞☞

In Monday's S.R. lesson, Nick presents a schedule
of all the breakfast, lunch and after-school clubs
where we can target voters. The Honey Badgers are
strong on both Sport and Culture, and Environment,
which means we need to woo every club going
with our other policies so they don't notice we've
allocated them a tiny part of the final budget.
Policy and Research work out which policies
will work for which groups, while Media and the
Treasurers divvy up leaflets and posters.

"And what's Jade going to do?" Coxy says, giving
me and Nick a side-eye. "Create a political scandal
by getting off with her campaign manager?"

I get there before Nick does. "Save your mud-
slinging for the opposition, Matthew Cox. This
candidate's staying squeaky clean all the way to
polling day."

Afterwards, though ...

"So," I say to Nick, who's trying to pretend he's cool with Coxy winding him up, "what you got for me?"

He hands me a schedule. "Tick whichever ones you can make."

And, without missing a beat, I tick all of them and hand it back to him. "Lunch is for losers. In it to win it, right?"

It's hard at first. Everything feels forced, but after I've got into the groove, I realise that I'm good at this. Names aren't my strong point, but everyone I stop is someone I've talked to before, maybe in orchestra practice or on the bus, or on the bench during a long-ago Year 8 hockey match. Or maybe it's someone I've only ever spoken to on a sofa in Starbucks. Whoever they are, I go for it. Even Rob King gets a neon orange Wildcat sticker pressed onto his shirt.

"You want my vote now, do you?" Rob asks, giving me a sly look.

"I want everyone's vote," I say, slapping stickers on all his friends, rolling my eyes like the whole thing's a total cheese-fest.

I might be serious about this, but I wouldn't want anyone to actually *know* that.

As I move onto a group of Year 10s, I catch sight of Stef, who gives me a smile and crafty thumbs-up.

"But I'm still voting for my sister," Stef says.

It's not until Thursday lunchtime that I end up with Nick, targeting the D&D gamers hiding in their corner of the library. Nick speaks their language when it comes to warlocks and whatnot, so I leave him to it, and head for some girls huddled round a jammed printer. It's the perfect excuse to give them Wildcat leaflets and our guff about funds to pay for a new printer for the library.

Nick's leaning against an Amnesty poster by the door, waiting for me.

"I didn't think you were all that serious about this," he says.

"You mean because Becky's the serious one, not me?"

"What's it got to do with Becky?" Nick's confused face is pretty adorable. "It's just you didn't seem that bothered at the hustings."

I feel a sudden need to adjust the ribbons on my rosette.

"I didn't prepare very much," I admit, not looking at him. "At all, in fact."

"OK, well ..." Nick clears his throat and starts edging about. "Umm ... if you wanted to, then, if you're free later I could, er, help prepare you for the debate tomorrow?"

👍 Second Best Friend 👎

✗

I find Becky by the lockers, wrestling with the landslide of Honey Badger leaflets she just knocked over with her History books. I nab one for research purposes.

"You don't mind skipping tonight, do you? I'm seeing you tomorrow anyway," I say. "I need to work on my arguments for the debate."

"Oh." Which is all Becky needs to say for me to know that she does mind.

I'm ready for this.

"It's just, after the mess I made of the hustings, I'm hoping to claw back a bit of dignity."

Becky nods, busy growling at the contents of her locker.

"Hey, Stickland." Nick passes by. "Catch you later."

I permit myself one extra second of watching Nick walk away before I turn to Becky, who's giving me an odd look.

"So it's the sort of debate prep you can do with Nick Pallis, but not with me?"

"Well, yeah, he's my campaign manager, you're …"

"The leader of the opposition, I know." Becky goes quiet a moment, digging about in her locker even though she's got the leaflets under control. Then she sighs and gives me a tired smile. "I'm also your best mate. You could have just said you wanted some alone time with Nick."

11
The Debate

Since the Wildcats are the more left-wing of the two parties, Nick and I agree that my speech should focus on equality. After we've polished my speech so much that the words slide smoothly from my mouth, we spend ten minutes with Nick firing questions at me like we're on *Question Time*.

"So do you think I'm ready, then?" I lean on the doorframe and tuck my hair behind my ear as I see Nick out. Debate prep has left me the same kind of restless as when I've been getting my flirt on, but for all Becky thinks that this was just an excuse to get with Nick, debate prep is all we've done.

"Put it this way – I'm glad *I'm* not up against you," Nick says.

"In the debating sense?" I add with a grin.

He grins back, eyes dipping down to my lips, where I'm biting back another tease. Nick Pallis *so* wants to kiss me. But Harvey comes stomping down the stairs behind me and Nick takes enough of a step back that my step-brother won't see anything worth teasing me about.

"So, um, will I see you at Raji's party tomorrow?" Nick asks.

"You'll see me at school," I say, smiling so he knows I'm playing with him. I have every intention of going to Raji's party.

"Here's to my victory tomorrow!" I hold up my hand for a very platonic high-five.

"To *our* victory," Nick says as he slaps my hand goodbye.

⚘⚘ Second Best Friend ⚘⚘

As I close the door, I frown at his correction.

✗

Turn-out for the debate isn't as good as it was for the hustings, but that's what you get if you hold it in the library over lunchtime. It's a bit of a downer, looking across a room a quarter full of people eating lunch off their knees. Becky shuffles her notes and gives me a weak smile as Mr Wilkinson bounds up to introduce us.

"The Wildcats and the Honey Badgers have canvassed hard this week, but today, Party Leaders Jade Stickland and Rebecca Conway have prepared final arguments to win your vote. After that, we'll have ten minutes for any pressing political questions. Jade, if you please …"

The hustings might have been a belly flop off

the bottom board at the local pool, but I've prepared
for today like it's the Olympic final.

Time to Tom Daley this debate.

"The Wildcats are a people-first party." Just like
when I was in the Debate Team I'm doing this from
memory. "Which means placing what *you* want
ahead of what the school thinks is best. Instead
of focusing investment on facilities, we intend to
spend our budget on what matters most – you,
the students. We are the party of the people, and
people are at the heart of our policies."

So many 'people' and 'policies'. For a second I'm
lost.

"Policies ..." *Shit.* "Policies ..." Nick is mouthing
the word *inclusive* at me. "That are inclusive. The
Wildcats propose drastic changes to the menu in
the canteen ..."

And that's it, I've hit my stride. I roll off all

the things I've been talking about this week into soundbites and jokes and deliver them with clarity and passion. As I approach the grand finish – the crowd pleaser – I know I've nailed this.

"A school that places so much importance on the value of words and ideas should place less on how people dress! If girls can wear skirts, boys can wear shorts. Bare legs for all!"

When I raise my fist, I feel just a tiny bit revolutionary.

✗

Later, in the S.R. lesson that follows, Nick turns round in his desk. "Well, you kinda rocked that, didn't you?"

"All thanks to my superstar campaign manager," I say. I give him a meaningful look and get one of his off-kilter grins in reply.

"Perhaps if Mr Pallis was facing the front he might realise that I asked him a question," Mr Wilkinson says in a voice so loud that even Nick, who isn't easily shamed, spins round with a sheepish look.

After Nick's presented the plan for polling day on Monday, Willow goes up to review the data her team has gathered. She takes the clicker from Mr Wilkinson and pulls a face.

"So, what we do is poll for voter intent, which means asking people who they think they'll vote for, so it's basically all just made up ..."

"Willow." Mr Wilkinson shakes his head to stall that line of thinking.

With a sigh that makes it clear she doesn't want to be there, Willow presses the button on the clicker. A three-bar graph appears, with a black bar marked 'H.B.', an orange one marked 'W.C.' and a grey one with 'Don't know'. The Honey Badger bar is nearly twice as long as the Wildcats bar.

"This was after the hustings," Willow says, giving me an apologetic look as I sit there, my face still, telling myself this isn't a surprise. "Which shows just how much ground our campaign gained this week."

She clicks through to the next graph – and I stare at it, feeling numb. The Honey Badgers still lead by over ten points.

12
Party Hard

The moment Dr Foong releases us from the Biology lab last lesson, Raji loops her arm in mine.

"I'm seeing you later, yeah? At the party?" There's a hint of worry in the way she looks at me, like she thinks I'm going to say no.

"Of course!" I squeeze her arm. "Your party's the only thing that's kept me going today."

Not an exaggeration – I'm in serious need of some fun.

Raji turns and grins at me as she skips forward to check who else is in, leaving me to walk with Becky.

After a few steps, Becky says, "I thought we agreed to stay in?"

"Did we? I don't remember that."

"Yesterday. When you ditched me for Nick, you said, 'I'll see you tomorrow anyway.'"

"Well, yeah. At Raji's party."

"I'm not up for a party. Not after all this election stuff –"

"The very reason we need a party!"

Becky shrinks inside her uniform. "Jade, I've been full beam for five days and I've run out of battery. All I want to do is stay home and hang out with my best friend – recharge."

The exact opposite of what I want.

Tonight I want to dance like my feet are on fire, find my campaign manager and cause a political scandal. I want to laugh at other people's jokes in the hope that I can remember to laugh at myself. I want a night where I can pretend I'm anyone other than Becky Conway's best friend.

"I need a night out. You need a night in," I say. I don't look at her as I add, "We can have both those things. Just not with each other."

✗

Back home I find a *Songs for When You Want to Punch Things* playlist on Spotify and crank it up as loud as it will go. There's a lot of Becky's influence in my wardrobe, but the look I want right now is a world away from my usual cute prints. I want to look angry and edgy and sexy.

By the time I'm done the girl in the mirror reflects the way I feel inside. My red hair's tousled like a rock star's, the most epic cat-flicks lining my eyes and even though my look isn't dressy, my vest clings in the right places and the neckline skims the top of my bra. I put a jumper over the top so Dad won't comment.

He still does.

"You've made a lot of effort for a night watching telly with your old man," he says when I go hunting in the kitchen for my scarf.

"I'm going out," I tell him. "Raji Grover's having a party."

Dad deadpans me over his laptop. "I worked that one out for myself." He twists round and passes me the scarf off the back of his chair. "Are you staying at Becky's again?"

"Becky's not coming out."

Dad looks like he thinks there's something wrong with that, but he can't work out what. "And you're not staying in with her?"

"No!" I yell, as I tug the end of my scarf too

tight. "God. Why does everyone assume I want to do everything that Becky does?"

Dad holds his hands up in surrender. "Whoa there, angry pants. If I was making an assumption I wouldn't have asked a question, would I? If you're not staying at Becky's, I'll come and get you. Quarter to midnight." Then he picks up a pen. "What's the postcode?"

✕

Raji's brother Priyam is in Year 10 and the Grovers' hall is crammed with boys who haven't yet worked out how to make cool look effortless. I add my scarf and jumper to the heap at the bottom of the stairs and catch sight in the mirror of the Year 10 boys giving me a totally unsubtle once-over.

Good to know I look as fierce as I feel.

"Jade!" Raji flings her arms up and sloshes whatever's in her glass onto the floor as I enter the huge kitchen-diner. Even as she hugs me, I can tell she's scouting round for Becky.

"She's not here," I say before Raji can ask.

"Ah, boo, how come?"

I can't stop myself. "Because she's too boring," I say.

I roll my eyes and grin and it works. Raji laughs along. "Yeah, I know what you mean!"

This isn't the response I expected and I stumble for something else to say. I latch onto the drink in her hand.

"What's that?" I ask.

13

Political Scandal

Archers and lemonade smells like a sherbet lemon got so drunk it vomited into a glass. It's the exact sort of thing my best friend thinks is vile. But without Becky around to draw me into a quiet corner and out of the crowd, I find myself two cups down and sucked into a massive group of people I only half know from school.

"Aren't you that girl on all those Wildcat posters?" a girl with the most amazing nail art asks me.

I take a sip of my drink and nod. "You gonna vote for me?"

"Give me one good reason why …"

Before I can answer, someone who smells delicious puts his arm round me and says, "Because she's the best candidate."

I'm already grinning when I look round to say hello to Nick – although I have to fight hard to keep my face straight when I see he's wearing a tweed waistcoat. Over a T-shirt.

The fact that I don't straight off call him a wanker can only mean one thing – I *definitely* fancy him.

Nick merges into our mismatched group as the conversation moves on to what Olympic sport we'd compete in if fitness and talent didn't matter. When Nick picks croquet, there's a lot of piss-taking that moves easily onto the outfit he's sporting. Instead of getting all argy-bargy about it the way Rob would have done, Nick leans right into it.

"Taking my style tips from Mr Wilkinson," he says, which makes a few people laugh, but it's me Nick's watching for a reaction. "I'm saving up for some two-tone winkle pickers and a silk cravat."

He's funny and I like him and I want to kiss him. And when someone else from our S.R. shouts at us to pose for a photo like the winners we are, I leave my arm round his waist a little longer than necessary.

As soon as the moment arises, all it takes is a lingering look and a raise of my eyebrows, and Nick's right behind me as I push open one of the doors that lead off the kitchen.

"Have you brought me to the laundry room?" he asks, as I shut the door after him. Given that there's a washing machine in the corner and a rack of damp clothes hanging over our heads, it would be hard to argue otherwise.

"Fancy a political scandal?" I say – and Nick closes the space between us so fast that he's not finished saying, "Absolutely!" before his lips are on mine and the tension from the last couple of weeks spills over into a kiss.

No fish breath, and when I run my fingers across the back of his head, his hair feels gorgeous. It's the kind of kiss that blocks out the rest of the world. Maybe seconds or minutes or hours later, I press Nick back against the edge of the sink and run my hands up under his T-shirt.

But he breaks away, flustered.

"Please don't think I'm not up for this, but maybe not right under another family's underwear?"

I follow his gaze up and wish I hadn't. No one needs to know what bra someone else's mum wears.

"Why don't we get back to the party for a bit?"

He twists his fingers in mine, tugs me to him for a quick kiss on the lips. "And look for somewhere more suitable for further political discussions?"

It's cute. *He's* cute.

"Sure," I say, pulling him closer. "In a minute."

And we're kissing once more, hotter and heavier than before, as if Nick's kissing away all the hurt and bitterness and jealousy that Rob stirred up. It's not top marks in a test, it's not a solo on the flute, it's not the biggest percentage of the electorate. It's not even 114 likes on Instagram. But if one like from a guy who thinks I'm hot is what's on offer, I'm going to take it.

Except Nick stops again.

"Jade." He's flushed and breathless. "This is awesome – I mean you're so – but ..."

"What?" He might be adorable, but this stop-start stuff is starting to get on my nerves.

"I think we should head back."

"Why?"

"I mean ..." He glances back at the door. "I feel bad about ditching my friends so early on. You know what I mean, right? Becky'll be wondering where you've got to ..."

14

Anger Mismanagement

I lose. My shit. All over the place.

"Oh my GOD!" I yell in Nick's face. "Am I not allowed to exist without Becky around? How did hooking up with *me* become about *her?*"

"What? Where's this coming from?" Nick looks desperate.

"It's coming from the fact that even when she's not in the same building as me, somehow she's all anyone wants to talk about!"

"I don't want to talk about her –" Nick insists.

"So why bring her up?"

"Have you two had a fight or something?" he says.

I'm slow to answer. Does what happened earlier count as a fight? But before I can work it out, Nick's gaze grows steady, as if something's just clicked.

"Is it about that stupid polling data?"

I say nothing, focusing on a spot on his waistcoat. HIS TWEED WAISTCOAT. Who does he think he is – Fantastic Mr Fox?

"Don't let that get to you." Nick gives my arm a gentle squeeze. "You come out top of the polls with me."

The politics chat has stopped being cute and Nick's turned into just another boy who wants to prove a point.

"Whatever, Nick. Just leave it."

But boys who think they know it all never do.

"No one thinks Becky's better than you –"

"Yes they do," I snap. "Dr Foong, Miss Cortez, 19% of the electorate, my own dad ..."

"What *are* you talking about?" It's probably best Nick interrupted before I mentioned Instagram. "So Becky's better at school, science, music ... So what? Grading a piece of homework isn't about grading a person. I got 82% in my last English Lit essay. Does that make me better than you too?"

He's trying to tease me out of my mood and his lips curl up the way that I've been craving all week, but I've pushed us beyond that now.

"No one compares me to *you*," I say.

"The only person who compares you to Becky is *you*."

"Just because you don't compare me to my best mate doesn't mean no one else does," I say, sounding as bitter as I feel. "You might think you're the voice of a generation, but you're just one person, Nick."

Nick takes his hand from my arm.

"Name one person, Jade." His voice has changed. "Just one who's compared you to Becky."

"Rob." The second I say it, I know I shouldn't have.

Nick stares at me, a blush blotching up his cheeks. His ears stick out in the cutest way and his hair's scuffed up from where I ran my fingers through it. I pick up on these details because I can't look him in the eye.

"So that ass-hat's opinion matters more than mine?" he says. "Rob King compared you to Becky, so now everyone does. I might not be the voice of a generation, but Rob King of the Twats is?"

"That's not –"

"I say one thing and Rob says – what?" Nick asks.

"I don't –"

"What?" Nick presses. "What did he say to mess you up like this?"

"He said he only got with me because Becky wasn't interested."

Nick crumbles, just a bit, and I think that maybe it's because he understands why that would cut me so deep. Maybe he'll forgive me for being so petty and irrational.

But when I dare to meet his eye, forgiveness isn't what I see.

"I was interested in you, Jade. Just you," Nick says.

Was.

And, with that, my last chance of winning walks out the door.

15

Dawn

When Dad knocks on my bedroom door and shouts for me to get up, it's like he's rapping his knuckles on the inside of my skull. I roll over and pull the duvet up and over my head.

Ugh. I stink.

And I'm shattered. I haven't slept well. It feels like I've been up all night partying even though I've been asleep for ... I check the clock – TWELVE HOURS? I sit up so fast it makes me dizzy and check my phone in case my clock's stopped, but nope, it's midday.

No wonder Dad's trying to get me out of bed.

There's tons of notifications on my phone, pictures I've been tagged in, messages I've missed ...

It makes me feel sick to look at them. Memories of what I did merge with the night's trippy dreams and fear frosts my insides.

Fear of what?

Most of the chats I'm a part of are nonsense – there's a long chain between me and Raji and Kirsten that's just us taking pictures of the Year 10s in the lounge and rating their terrible dance moves. Among the chats is a message from Nick.

Sorry about before. Can we talk?

It's been opened, but I didn't reply and I can't remember talking to him.

There's also a short chain between me and Becky that ends just after ten.

I SNOGGED NICK.

Hello???

Are you there?

Sorry, was having a bath. Not surprised about Nick. Sounds like you're having a good time.

I'M HAVING THE BEST TIME. Plus six different excitable emojis.

Good to know. I'm off to bed now.

Night night, Grandma.

Still uneasy, I open up Instagram. In fact, I feel sick, like there's something I'm looking for that I know is there but don't want to see. The sickness grows worse as I check several different tags, as if the next one will reveal something dreadful.

There's a picture of me with my arm round some boy I don't know, mashing a kiss into the side of his face. We're both doing the Wildcat claw strike and his comment is *@jadedbabe has my vote #VoteWildcat #Rawr* etc.

We started #VoteWildcat as part of the

campaign, but everything tagged #VoteWildcat in the last few hours is me with randoms from the party pulling increasingly stupid faces.

As I scroll through them, I start to feel a swell of relief. Sure, I'm cringing now to see these in the sober light of day and not through the filter of who-knows-how-many drinks and a lot of loud music, but behaving like an idiot about an election no one else cares about is just stupid, not anything to be scared of.

Regret punctures my relief when I get to the last of the pictures – the first one of the night. Me and Nick, posing like the winners we are.

116 likes – and one of them was Nick.

✗

Dad watches me as I fall on my sausages and mash like I've not eaten for a week.

"Good night last night?" he says.

I nod. Now I'm clean and dressed and eating, the dread I woke up with is fading.

"Mm ... smelled like it when you got in the car." I stop chewing and stare at him. "Yes, Jade. Your old man knows when his daughter's been drinking. You're very talkative when you're tipsy."

I start chewing again because I don't know what to say.

"This isn't something I expected from you." He sighs and glances across the table to Mandy and Harvey. They look a lot like they wish they weren't here. "I thought you were more responsible."

"I'm sorry, Dad," I say. He's not impressed.

"I'm going to have to have a word with Becky's parents if this is –"

"No," I say, in a rush. "It isn't! We never drink when we're out. I promise."

Dad nods. "So it's only Becky who's more responsible?"

I wait, expecting to feel the familiar flare of anger at the constant comparison, but I don't. All I feel is dread. There's something I've forgotten. Something terrible – and it has to do with Becky.

"... not what I expect of my daughter ..."

What? What is it I've done? Why can't I remember?

"... can't set your own boundaries ..."

I can't remember much. After Nick ditched me in the laundry room, I kind of went for it.

"... grounded."

Dad's words finally hit me.

"*What?*"

"You're grounded, Jade," he states. "You're not to see anyone this weekend, or the next. Now hand me your phone."

🧡 Second Best Friend 🧡

Dazed, I take my phone out of my pocket, ready to hand it over ... then snatch it back just as Dad's about to grasp it.

"No!" I say, as panic spills out of me. "I can't, please, Dad?" I remember now what it is that I've done. "Please, Dad, I've got to check something –"

"Jade!" He's not happy about any of this and he snaps his fingers for the phone. "Don't be ridiculous. Whatever it is can't be that important if you've only just remembered."

Only it is. It's the most important thing ever.

It was late. Someone had suggested we whisper secrets round the circle of people sitting on the kitchen floor. There were six of us – Raji and her brother, two other Year 10s, Kirsten. I was sitting next to ... A boy. He smelled like a toffee apple and I'd wondered if that was what he'd taste like if I licked him.

Shame balloons up when I remember I kissed him after that, but it's nothing compared to the suffocating horror I feel at what I told him, why I got close enough to smell him.

My lips brushed his ear as I gave away the biggest secret that wasn't mine to tell.

Becky Conway once lied about having cancer.

16
Gotta Get Away

For the rest of the weekend I'm trapped in the house fretting about what I've done, knowing there's nothing I can do to stop the fallout.

The phone ban is the worst kind of torture. It leaves me no option but to run and re-run the memory of the secret I told. The enormity of my betrayal grows with every replay. But it's not like having my phone could change that, is it? The only way for this to be fixed would be for it never to happen. I might have got an upgrade, but it's an iPhone, not a time machine. Even Apple haven't worked that one out yet.

On Sunday, I cry myself to sleep. I beg the universe to help, praying that it can stop Becky from finding out what I've done.

"Here." Dad reaches across the table at breakfast and hands me back my phone. "It's fully charged."

I stare at the screen, sick so far beyond my stomach I can feel it in my bones.

"Thanks," I say. My throat is dry at the sight of how many notifications there are on my lock screen. I skim through them, my breath held so tight it might strangle me.

But there's nothing nuclear on there.

My fingers tremble as I check the millions of messages from Becky, each more stressed out than the last.

Jade??? Is everything OK??? Really worried I've pissed you off or something. And then there's a string of anxious emojis.

The bottom drops out of my world as I realise she doesn't know. All this weekend, Becky hasn't been hating me, she's been missing me.

I hammer back a reply, my thumbs a blur.

OH MY GOD I'm so sorry!!! MY DAD TOOK MY PHONE BECAUSE I GOT DRUNK AT THE PARTY?!?!?! You TOTALLY haven't pissed me off in any way whatsoever.

I send it, then type another.

You are the best friend ever and I'm so sorry for freaking you out xxxxxxxxxxxx

And then I have to run to the bathroom so I don't burst into tears in front of my family.

At school I'm so aggressively nice to Becky that she tells me to cut it out.

"It's only because I've missed you," I say, not quite looking at her.

"Two days, Jade!" Becky laughs at me. "I reckon our friendship can survive that."

And when she holds a hand up for the Fist Bump of Friendship, I take care not to look at anyone else. The relief I feel at being back with Becky is masked by the knowledge that her secret is out there in other people's minds. It's like a shadow cast over our friendship that only I can feel.

In all of this, I'd forgotten about the election. Today is the day of the vote and I walk with Becky down to the foyer outside the school hall where both parties are doing some last minute canvassing. I really don't want to face Nick, but as he's the one who's organising us, it's not like I have a choice. He and I are meant to be staffing the Wildcats' table, and it's already covered in ribbons and leaflets and a bucket of penny sweets to tempt people to talk to us.

"Hey, Nick," I say, walking over, hands in pockets, trying not to show how crushingly awkward this is.

"Here." Nick hands me a Wildcat rosette and a bucket of sweets, but before I've even had a chance to put on my rosette, there's a crowd of Year 10 boys plunging their hands into the sweets.

"All right, Jade?" one of them says.

I look up to see Toffee Apple Boy.

Oh God. For a moment the horror of being faced with the fact that I kissed a Year 10 wipes out all my other problems.

"Hi." My mouth is as close to a smile as a strawberry lace is to a piece of fruit. "Vote Wildcats!"

Toffee Apple grins. "You got my vote on Friday, babe."

BABE.

I'd feel less sick if I tipped the whole bucket of sweets down my throat.

Nick stares at me as the boys walk off into the hall, but before he can say anything, I make a bolt for Willow. She's standing with a clipboard, collecting polling data from the people who've already voted.

"Willow. This is an emergency." She's my only hope. "Can you campaign with Nick? Please?"

Willow frowns at the sweets I'm handing her, then over at Nick.

"Did I miss something? I thought you guys pulled at the party?" But before I can explain she lets out a weary sigh and hands me the clipboard. "You could have waited until after the vote to go off him, Jade."

I should be offended, but instead I swap my sweets for her questionnaire.

👍 Second Best Friend 👎

Did you vote for the same party today that you would have voted for a week ago? Yes / No / Didn't know who to vote for.

If your answer was no, or you didn't know, what made you change your mind? Circle all that apply.

- *Policies – Environment / Health and Welfare / Sport and Culture / Student Rights*
- *Campaigning*
- *Leader performance in the debates*
- *Other (please specify)*

As a couple of Year 11 girls step out of the hall, I move forward.

"Excuse me, do you have a moment to answer these two questions?"

17
Moment of Truth

We have S.R. next and after a lesson spent sorting out the questionnaires Mr Wilkinson holds me and Nick back.

Confused, I glance over at Nick, but he refuses to look at me.

"Jade. Nick." Mr Wilkinson crosses his arms, looking serious. "It's come to my attention that the two of you have been involved with posting some, shall we say, *non-political* statements on the Vote Wildcat hashtag."

It's as if I've bitten off a mouthful of shame and swallowed it before I've had a chance to chew.

"This is not the sort of behaviour I would expect from either of you and I'm not sure how to deal with it." He looks like he expects us to help him.

"I'm sorry, sir," I say, trying not to think of all the photos he must have seen. "There was a party on Friday and I got a bit carried away in the ... erm ... spirit? Of the election?"

Mr Wilkinson doesn't look at all convinced.

"It won't happen again, sir," Nick says. "As Jade says, we're very sorry."

Mr Wilkinson lets us dangle a moment longer before letting out a huff. We get another five minutes of bollocking, but we leave the classroom without any official punishment.

Nick and I walk together to the library.

"I *am* sorry, you know," I say in a low voice.

"About abusing the hashtag?"

"About Friday. I shouldn't have taken my –"

I pause, not yet ready to admit what Nick saw

"– *issues* out on you."

Our pace has slowed to a crawl and I risk a look at Nick. He's not happy.

"I heard you spent the rest of the night seeing how much of your tongue Harry Webb could fit in his mouth, so I'm not sure that your sorry and my sorry are quite the same thing."

I guess Toffee Apple Boy has a name.

"It was just a party hook-up," I say, wishing it wasn't even that.

"Me or Harry?"

"Not you," I reply. I've kissed enough boys to know the difference between a one-off snog and something more meaningful.

Nick sighs and scuffs his heel on the floor as we pause outside the library. "I didn't think I stood a chance. You're well out of my league."

It's pathetic how my stomach flips over at a compliment like that.

"Maybe we could have two chances?" I say, and I feel a familiar fizz when I meet his gaze. "Sober. Without the smell of washing powder in the air."

Nick seems unsure, but his eyes smile, even if his mouth doesn't.

"OK," he says. "Maybe we could hang out after school. Starbucks or something?"

"Sure," I say, deciding to 'forget' that I'm grounded.

That done, Nick pushes the door of the library open for me. And I step right into a nightmare.

There, at a table by herself is my best friend. She's trying to hide the fact that she's crying.

My deepest, most craven instinct is to run away. To leave Becky there, surrounded by people who don't know her well enough to offer comfort, so that

I don't have to face the truth. But Nick is already crossing the room, crouching down to put an arm round her and asking if she's OK.

"What is it? What's happened?" he asks and I wait, wanting to hear it ...

Becky sits up and wipes her eyes on her sleeve and looks confused about why Nick is comforting her and not me.

"Something Stef said ..." Becky begins.

Relief sets me free and I have to force myself not to smile in the face of Becky's misery. They've had a fight. That's all. Nothing to do with me. Stef issues I can cope with.

I pull out a chair and take up my position as best friend, arm round Becky.

"What's she done?" I ask.

"Been an utter *bitch*." The shock of Becky swearing like that makes everyone within earshot flinch.

"I, er, do you need me to get you some tissues?" Nick offers. It's clear he doesn't want to get trapped in the middle of this, but Becky's not listening to him. She digs around in her pocket and pulls out a crumpled piece of paper.

It's one of the questionnaires from lunchtime and I'm aware of Nick's confused little frown as he leans over to read it. The person who filled it out changed their mind about who to vote for – and it was for 'other' reasons, not because of the policies.

"I can't believe she told them," Becky mutters through her teeth as she shakes with rage. "Why? Why would she do that? Oh God, I hate her ..."

All I can do is stare at the paper pressed flat on the table. I read the words over and over and over as a high-pitched whine of panic drowns out Nick's words and Becky's fresh tears.

I heard Becky Conway once lied about having cancer. No way can I vote for someone like her after that.

"It wasn't Stef," I whisper.

They don't hear me and, for a moment, I think I could stay quiet and let Stef take the blame. But I can't. If I don't tell Becky the truth now, someone else will.

"It wasn't Stef," I say again.

Nick looks up so sharply that I know he understands what I mean. His mouth tips down in a look of horror and distaste.

Becky, on the other hand, misses the point.

"Oh my God, Jade!" she snaps. "Can't you just take my side on this *one* thing? You don't always have to defend her!"

"What?" This isn't how this conversation was meant to go. "I don't – I'm not!"

"Oh really? Whenever I talk about Stef you always leap in to defend her –"

I'm confused and enlightened and sad all at the same time. Is that really how Becky sees it?

This has just become *so* much worse.

"Becky. Please," I say, and my voice cracks as it struggles to say what I need it to. "It was me. I told them. It wasn't Stef."

18

Consequences

Becky says nothing. Then she stands, picks her bag up and walks out. As I go to follow her, Nick grabs my arm and pulls me back.

"If she wanted to see you, she wouldn't have left."

I turn to him, stricken – I want him to tell me what I can do to make this right – but all he does is look as if I've shed my human form and emerged as a snake.

"What happened, Jade?" he asks. "I thought you were Becky's best friend?"

"I am," I say, but as the words leave my mouth they taste like a lie.

Second Best Friend

×

Once the last bell goes, I hang around the lockers to wait for Nick, but he doesn't show – just sends me a message.

Sorry to bail, but I don't think we should start anything right now. The last two weeks have been fun for me, but I get the sense they mean something different to you. You need to sort stuff with Becky.

I screw my eyes up and think about all the ways things have gone wrong. How it all started with listening to Rob King – not what he said, but how I reacted.

We all have our weak points. I just didn't know my best mate was mine.

Becky doesn't answer her phone or reply to the hundreds of messages I send, begging, grovelling, pleading for her to get in touch. I stop short of

going round her house and knocking on her door.
I could pretend it's because I'm grounded, but it's
because I don't dare risk running into Stef.

*"If she finds out I told you about the cancer that
never was, I'll kill you. Slowly. Painfully. Publicly."*

For all I confessed that I let the secret out,
Becky knows it's a secret that could only come from
one source.

Becky's off the next day, but her sister isn't and
Stef follows me into the toilet. When I hear her
stop outside the middle cubicle, my brain plays a
montage of my worst fears – Stef kicking down the
door, yanking me off the loo with my tights round
my ankles so she can press my cheek to the hand-
dryer and hiss threats into my ear.

That's not what happens. This is Clark
Academy, not an episode of *Orange Is The New
Black*.

"Jade?" Stef says. "I know you're in there."

"I am," I say. I'm holding in my wee, even though I'm desperate.

"What did you do?" The shadows shift under the door and there's a dull thump as Stef slumps against it.

"I'm sorry," I say.

"So?"

I don't have an answer for that.

"She won't talk to me," Stef says. "Mum Maria and Mally have both tried to find out what's wrong, but Becky won't budge."

Here was me thinking that, as the wronged party, Becky at least had the right to talk about it with anyone she wanted. But she can't tell her mums, can she? If she told them what's happened she'd have to confess to something she never wanted them to know.

"Open the door, Jade," Stef says and I think she might be crying.

"I need to, um ... y'know," I say.

"Go for it." Stef steps away and I rush out a wee, embarrassed that someone's listening. I sort myself out and open the door to find Stef, always so cool and composed, in bits by the sink.

Like everything else that has happened, it is so much worse than I imagined.

"Why, Jade?" Stef says, as she wipes her nose on the back of her hand. "Why did you tell everyone? I thought you cared about her."

"I don't know," I say.

How can I tell Stef that I was so desperate for my turn at the top that I pulled my best friend down to get there?

✗

🐾 Second Best Friend 🐾

There's no sign of Becky on Wednesday and during
S.R. Mr Wilkinson returns our analysis of the polling
data.

He hands mine back with a frown. "Didn't
put much effort into this one, did you?" He's not
expecting me to answer. The mark he's given me, I
don't need to.

I feel like crying. Everything I've done since
Rob taunted me with that comment about Becky has
been to prove that I'm better in any way I can, and
yet here I am, failing in the only subject I ever felt
good at.

"The results will be announced tomorrow in
assembly," Mr Wilkinson addresses the class. "I'd
like everyone to write me a review of who you
think will win and why. Refer back to polling data,
campaign plans and, of course, instinct. Everyone
except you, Jade."

That sentence makes me think of Rob reaching out to pat my cheek in the cinema.

"You need to prepare a winning speech, just in case. It would be nice to have some visuals to go with it, so perhaps Matthew Cox can set you up with a simple PowerPoint?"

I can't believe Mr Wilkinson is talking about this like it matters.

Everyone in the world could vote for me and it wouldn't make me a winner.

✗

Thursday's the same – no Becky – and the walk home without her feels all wrong. Then I remember I didn't walk home with her last week either, because I was with Nick.

The thought sends me spiralling into regret

again. It's like being forced down a helter-skelter on repeat, dizzying and tiring and tedious.

At home, I take out my S.R. folder and think about my homework as I flick over the notes I made on our campaign. There's nothing I feel less like doing than preparing a victory speech and – as always – I pick up my phone to distract me. I've not posted anything since Monday so there's no notifications and, after I've scrolled my feed, I find that re-gram of me and Becky, the one we both posted before I turned toxic from the inside out.

I spend a long, long time staring at the two of us on my phone. Long enough that it fades to lock screen. Then I put my phone down and I write my speech.

19

A Sorry Speech

Becky comes to school. She doesn't speak to me, doesn't even look at me. But she's here. When Becky asks Willow if she can sit with her in form time, Willow just moves her bag off the chair and pats the seat, darting a glance at me.

Like everyone else, Willow's hazy on the details of our fight. The official story is that it's nothing more than a blow-up between the Conway twins, with me on the wrong side – but who knows what people might really believe if they've heard the cancer story? No one's confronted me about it, but that doesn't mean they aren't thinking it.

Even when the two of us are crammed on stage with the rest of our party reps, Becky still doesn't look my way. Mr Wilkinson steps up to the microphone and waffles on about the democratic process and academic goals. I catch phrases like "carefully planned" and "hotly contested" and "swing vote", but the only thing I'm listening for is the result.

For the first time since I was voted in as party leader, I've a good reason to win.

"The winner is *the Wildcat party* with a majority of twelve votes!"

There were six people in that kitchen who heard the cancer rumour. Six votes that didn't go to the Honey Badgers, six votes that went to the Wildcats. A majority of twelve ...

Down at the front, Miss Prasad opens up the PowerPoint marked 'Wildcat Win' – the one I made

without any help from Coxy – and the Wildcat logo
lights up the screen at the back of the stage.

I take the clicker and step up to the microphone,
aware of the rest of my party jumping up and down,
Coxy's yell of "Get in there!"

"Go Wildcats!" I call.

It's pretty feeble, but still everyone settles down.

"So." My voice sounds weird in the microphone.
"A majority of you voted for us. Thank you."

There are cheers from the crowd.

"Perhaps you were convinced by the Wildcats'
open and inclusive policies? Maybe it was the
vegetarian meals that swayed you?" I pause
and tap the clicker to show a picture of the best
chocolate cake I could find on Pinterest. "Or the
promise of better puddings?"

Everyone laughs at that one. Even the teachers.
It was a popular policy.

"But ..." I draw their focus back to me. "If you voted for the Wildcats because you liked *me*, then I'm sorry, but you made a mistake." A couple of people exchange puzzled looks. "Whoever you vote as your leader should have integrity, but when you compromise the people you love, you compromise yourself. And that is what I have done."

There's a murmur of confusion among the crowd and Nick steps forward to lay a hand on my arm.

"Jade ..."

I shrug him off. The only person I care about right now is Becky.

"Becky Conway has always been my best friend," I say, "but recently I was tricked into seeing her as something else. My better friend."

I press the clicker again and the stupid chocolate cake is replaced by the selfie of me and

Becky that I've been so hung up on. Across from me, Becky's hands are up, masking most of her face, but she's staring up at the photo like everyone else.

"It's an easy trap to fall into. We're measured against each other all the time – not just me and Becky, but all of us. From top grades to the bottom of the class, who scored the most goals in the last match, who gets picked to represent the school. It's not like it stops when we walk out the gates. Our outfit of the day, our new lipstick, our sense of humour – they can all be measured in little red hearts on Instagram."

When I press the clicker the picture splits in two – Becky's covered in 114 little red hearts, mine in 54.

"A measure of my selfie felt too much like a measure of my *self* – yet another way in which my best friend was better."

I pause and swallow, aware that Miss Prasad and Mr Wilkinson are having a very heated discussion about whether they should stop my speech there.

"This election was a chance to change things. A chance to win. All I wanted was to come first for once. But everything I did to prove I was the best only made things worse."

Mr Wilkinson's made a decision. He's out of his seat and up the steps at the side of the stage. I've got to be fast.

"Last Friday, I spread a rumour about Becky Conway because I wanted to win –"

"Jade, come away now ..." Mr Wilkinson says.

"– and that is not the action of a leader, but a loser."

Mr Wilkinson tries to cover the microphone, but I brush him off.

"*Let me finish*," I hiss. "Who knows if Becky Conway is the better candidate, but she's 100% the better person. She isn't the liar. I am. And I'm sorry."

As soon as I stop, Mr Wilkinson ushers me away into the wings, from where I can hear the whole school erupt into feverish gossip.

For anyone in Years 7 to 9 most of what I said won't have made any sense at all. They barely know who Becky is, let alone what rumours are flying around about her.

"There's clearly a lot more to this than I realised," Mr Wilkinson murmurs and frowns down at me as I sit on the Wizard of Oz throne. "Would you care to explain what on earth's been going on, Jade?"

I shake my head.

Mr Wilkinson sighs. "This is not the learning

outcome I was looking for ... first the hashtag, now this." He points at me like I'm a naughty puppy. "Stay here. I need to help Miss Prasad out."

He darts back onto the stage. I watch the heavy curtains sway in his wake and then I collapse forward, head in hands, every muscle in my body feeling the strain as I hope so hard that it hurts.

I wish I'd never listened to Rob, who is nothing more than a small boy trying to make himself feel bigger. I wish I'd known better than to feed my jealousy with comparisons no one but me made.

Most of all, I wish my best friend was here.

The boards creak, like someone's approaching, but I keep my head down, face hidden, not wanting Mr Wilkinson to see what a mess I am. Only it can't be Mr Wilkinson, because whoever it is sits down on the arm of the throne and lays a hand on my back. Whoever it is smells of fabric softener and the Marc

Jacobs tester that smelled nicer on Becky than it did me.

"Jade?" she says.

I open my eyes and look up at my best friend.

I NEVER REALLY BELIEVED
IT WOULD COME TO THIS
DEATH WAS SOMETHING THAT
HAPPENED IN OTHER
PEOPLE'S STORIES
NOT MINE
NOT MILLIE'S

Unboxed

Non Pratt

Acknowledgements

Second Best Friend is a book born of my own insecurities – ones I've (mostly) overcome thanks to all the writers I call friends. There really are too many to list, but if you're reading this wondering whether I mean you, then I probably do.

More specific gratitude to @ChouettBlog @books_polished and @tara1966 for Willow's hair and @LeanneWain and Archie Hamerton who were kind enough to explain the mysteries of school timetabling.

I do so love my Barrington Stoke crew – Emma, Jane, Julie-ann, Kirstin and Nina – the Bounce team too. Yet again, I have been blessed with Kate Alizadeh's hand-lettering and artwork, please do go check out www.katealizadeh.net. You won't regret it.

Thank you to Alysia McDonagh – the kind of friend who inspires me to do better without ever making me feel worse. And for letting me borrow your daughter's name.

And Pragmatic Dan, I am always grateful.

Are you a book eater or a book avoider — or something in between?

This book is designed to help more people love reading. It's witty, unflinching, astute – an utterly contemporary story of friendship, self-discovery and politics by a fantastic author. There's a stunning cover, shiny foil and more for book lovers to treasure. At the same time, it has clever design features to support more readers.

You may notice the book is printed on heavy paper in two colours – black for the text and a pale yellow Pantone® for the page background. This reduces the contrast between text and paper and hides the 'ghost' of the words printed on the other side of the page. For readers who perceive blur or movement as they read, this may help keep the text still and clear. The book also uses a unique typeface that is dyslexia-friendly.

If you're a book lover, and you want to help spread the love, try recommending *Second Best Friend* to someone you know who doesn't like books. You never know – maybe a super-readable book is all they need to spark a lifelong love of reading.